More Munsch to Enjoy!

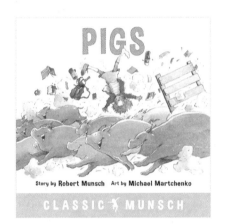

PIGS

Story by **Robert Munsch** Art by **Michael Martchenko**

CLASSIC MUNSCH

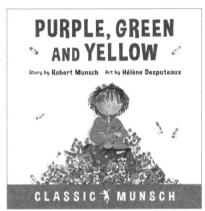

PURPLE, GREEN AND YELLOW

Story by **Robert Munsch** Art by **Hélène Desputeaux**

CLASSIC MUNSCH

The Paper Bag Princess

Story by **Robert Munsch** Art by **Michael Martchenko**

CLASSIC MUNSCH

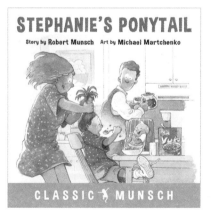

STEPHANIE'S PONYTAIL

Story by **Robert Munsch** Art by **Michael Martchenko**

CLASSIC MUNSCH

We acknowledge the support of the Canada Council for the Arts and the Ontario Arts Council, and the participation of the Government of Canada/la participation du gouvernement du Canada for our publishing activities.

Library and Archives Canada Cataloguing in Publication

Munsch, Robert N., 1945-, author
    Thomas' snowsuit / Robert Munsch ; illustrated by Michael
Martchenko. – Classic Munsch edition.

Originally published in 1985.
ISBN 978-1-77321-038-4 (hardcover).--ISBN 978-1-77321-037-7 (softcover)

    I. Martchenko, Michael, illustrator II. Title.

PS8576.U575T5 2018   jC813'.54   C2017-905738-3

Published in the U.S.A. by Annick Press (U.S.) Ltd.
Distributed in Canada by University of Toronto Press.
Distributed in the U.S.A. by Publishers Group West.

Printed in China

www.annickpress.com
www.robertmunsch.com

Also available in e-book format. Please visit www.annickpress.com/ebooks.html for more details.

Thomas' Snowsuit

STORY by
ROBERT MUNSCH

ART by
MICHAEL MARTCHENKO

annick press
toronto • berkeley

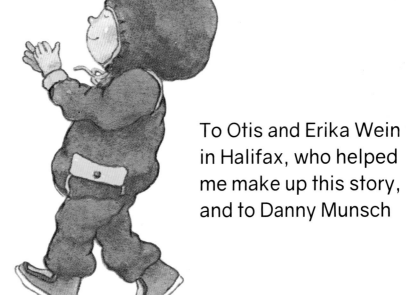

To Otis and Erika Wein
in Halifax, who helped
me make up this story,
and to Danny Munsch

One day, Thomas' mother bought him a nice new brown snowsuit. When Thomas saw that snowsuit he said, "That is the ugliest thing I have ever seen in my life. If you think that I am going to wear that ugly snowsuit, you are crazy!"

Thomas' mother said, "We will see about that."

The next day, when it was time to go to school, the mother said, "Thomas, please put on your snowsuit," and Thomas said,

"NNNNNO."

His mother jumped up and down and said, "Thomas, put on that snowsuit!"

And Thomas said, "*NNNNNO!*"

So Thomas' mother picked up Thomas in one hand, picked up the snowsuit in the other hand, and she tried to stick them together. They had an enormous fight, and when it was done Thomas was in his snowsuit.

Thomas went off to school and hung up his snowsuit. When it was time to go outside, all the other kids jumped into their snowsuits and ran out the door. But not Thomas.

The teacher looked at Thomas and said, "Thomas, please put on your snowsuit."

Thomas said, "**NNNNNO.**"

The teacher jumped up and down and said, "Thomas, put on that snowsuit."

And Thomas said, "**NNNNNO.**"

So the teacher picked up Thomas in one hand, picked up the snowsuit in the other hand, and she tried to stick them together. They had an enormous fight, and when they were done the teacher was wearing Thomas' snowsuit and Thomas was wearing the teacher's dress.

When the teacher saw what she was wearing, she picked up Thomas in one hand and tried to get him back into his snowsuit. They had an enormous fight. When they were done, the snowsuit and the dress were tied into a great big knot on the floor and Thomas and the teacher were in their underclothes.

Just then the door opened, and in walked the principal. The teacher said, "It's Thomas. He won't put on his snowsuit."

The principal gave his very best PRINCIPAL LOOK
and said, "Thomas, put on your snowsuit."

And Thomas said, "NNNNNO."

So the principal picked up Thomas in one hand and he picked up the teacher in the other hand, and he tried to get them back into their clothes. When he was done, the principal was wearing the teacher's dress, the teacher was wearing the principal's suit, and Thomas was still in his underwear.

Then from far out in the playground someone yelled, "Thomas, come and play!" Thomas ran across the room, jumped into his snowsuit, got his boots on in two seconds, and ran out the door.

The principal looked at the teacher and said, "Hey, you have on my suit. Take it off right now."

The teacher said, "Oh, no. You have on my dress. You take off my dress first."

Well, they argued and argued and argued, but neither one wanted to change first.

Finally, Thomas came in from recess. He looked at the principal and he looked at the teacher. Thomas picked up the principal in one hand. He picked up the teacher in the other hand. They had an enormous fight and Thomas got everybody back into their clothes.

The next day the principal quit his job and
moved to Arizona, where nobody ever
wears a snowsuit.

Even More Classic Munsch:

The Dark
Mud Puddle
The Paper Bag Princess
The Boy in the Drawer
Jonathan Cleaned Up, Then He Heard a Sound
Millicent and the Wind
Mortimer
The Fire Station
Angela's Airplane
David's Father
50 Below Zero
I Have to Go!
Moira's Birthday
A Promise is a Promise
Pigs
Something Good
Show and Tell
Purple, Green and Yellow
Wait and See
Where is Gah-Ning?
From Far Away
Stephanie's Ponytail
Munschworks: The First Munsch Collection
Munschworks 2: The Second Munsch Treasury
Munschworks 3: The Third Munsch Treasury
Munschworks 4: The Fourth Munsch Treasury
The Munschworks Grand Treasury
Munsch Mini-Treasury One
Munsch Mini-Treasury Two
Munsch Mini-Treasury Three

For information on these titles please visit www.annickpress.com
Many Munsch titles are available in French and/or Spanish, as well as in
board book and e-book editions. Please contact your favorite supplier.

More Munsch to Enjoy!

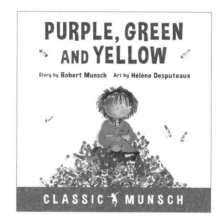

PURPLE, GREEN AND YELLOW

Story by Robert Munsch   Art by Hélène Desputeaux

CLASSIC ✶ MUNSCH

PIGS

Story by Robert Munsch   Art by Michael Martchenko

CLASSIC ✶ MUNSCH

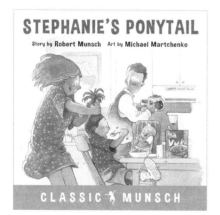

STEPHANIE'S PONYTAIL

Story by Robert Munsch   Art by Michael Martchenko

CLASSIC ✶ MUNSCH

The Paper Bag Princess

Story by Robert Munsch   Art by Michael Martchenko

CLASSIC ✶ MUNSCH